I hope you enjoy the book :)

D K

Dalis to the Rescue

by Dalis Hitchcock   illustrated by Veronica Montoya

Dalis to the Rescue • Michigan • USA

Acknowledgments

My thanks go to all of the many supporters who have believed in me every step of the way. To the donators, fosters, and adopters who help make Dalis to the Rescue possible. To the volunteers who help with the daily animal care. To Katherine, Angela, and Junie for being there for me every step of the way. To my amazing board members, Nicole Gorsuch and Maegan Fabiano, who have supported me from day one. To my wonderful sanctuary committee, Kate, Katherine, Kelli, and Jess.

To the many vets who believe in me and my passion for saving animals. To Dr. Rosetto, Dr. Langois, Dr. Gruca, and the two vets I named the vet in the book after, Dr. Kolesar and Dr. Cresswell ("Dr. KC"). Dr. Cresswell was the first vet I worked with, and was part of the reason I could save so many animals in the beginning. When Dr. Cresswell retired, I found Dr. Kolesar, who now helps me save so many injured animals. To all my vet techs who field my frantic calls and deal with my craziness with ease.

To my mom, dad, brother, and daughters, Junie and Modestie, who have always supported my crazy love for animals. And to my fiancé, David Garza. On the very first day we met, I told him there were two rules to dating me. First, he had to love my family no matter what, and second, he could never say no to me bringing home an animal, even if I already had a hundred (not knowing that one day I would actually have a hundred animals!). Seventeen years later, he is still my biggest supporter…and has never said no to any animals that I have brought home. He continues to let me be my true self by doing what I love to do, rescuing animals. Thank you all for your support.

For David, Junie, and Modestie,
my biggest supporters.
And for the millions of animals who have no voice.

D. H.

I want to thank the Book Bridge Press team
for giving me the opportunity to illustrate
Dalis to the Rescue, *a wonderful story*
about the connection between people and animals,
an authentic, wordless friendship.
The process of creating Dalis, a tender, strong girl,
and all of her friends has been a great experience.

—V. M.

Dalis to the Rescue
317 North Mill Street
St. Louis, Michigan 48880

www.dalistotherescue.com

First Edition
10 9 8 7 6 5 4 3 2 1

LCCN 2019940281
ISBN 978-0-578-50019-5

book bridge press

This book was proudly produced by Book Bridge Press.
www.bookbridgepress.com

Dalis had trouble making friends. The human kind, that is. Kids could be mean to Dalis. Sometimes they called her names or did not invite her to play. Dalis felt sad and lonely.

One day when Dalis was walking home after another hard day of school, she came upon a stray dog.

"Who are you?" Dalis asked.

"My name is Alfonzo," said the dog.

"What's wrong?" Dalis asked.

"I broke my leg, and now my family can't afford to take me to the vet to get it fixed. They are frustrated and have decided to give me up. Now I am looking for a new home," Alfonzo said. "What should I do?"

"Come along with me, and I'll see how I can help," Dalis said.

So along walked Dalis and Alfonzo, both looking a little less sad and alone.

All of a sudden, they came across a cat.

"Who are you?" Dalis asked.

"My name is Crooked Curt," said the cat. He looked very sad too.

"What's wrong?" Dalis asked.

"I have a disability that causes me to walk in circles. My owners didn't understand that overbreeding can cause health problems like mine. They didn't want me, and now I'm homeless. What should I do?"

"Come along with me, and I'll see how I can help," Dalis said.

So along walked Dalis, Alfonzo, and Crooked Curt, each looking a little less sad and lonely.

All of a sudden they came across a big green iguana.

"Who are you?" Dalis asked.

"My name is Elizabeth," the iguana said. She looked sad too.

"What's wrong?" Dalis asked.

"I wasn't properly cared for, but only by accident. My humans bought me from a pet store when I was a tiny baby, but they didn't know how to care for me. As I grew larger and larger, I got sicker and sicker, and now I don't know what to do."

"Well, Alfonzo has a broken leg, Crooked Curt has a disability, you are very sick, and I am very sad and lonely. Come along with us, and I'll see how I can help," Dalis said.

So along walked Dalis, Alfonzo, Crooked Curt, and Elizabeth, each looking a little less sad and lonely.

"Squawk!" They came across a beautiful bird.

"Who are you?" Dalis asked.

"My name is Sasha." She looked sad too.

"What's wrong?" Dalis asked.

Sasha said, "I was bought by my owners who didn't know very much about birds. They thought I was beautiful but didn't learn about what it takes to care for a bird. I was loud and messy, and would bite at times, so my owners decided to find a new home for me. What should I do?"

"Well, Alfonzo has a broken leg, Crooked Curt has a disability, Elizabeth is very sick, and you need a new home. Come along with us, and I'll see how I can help," Dalis said.

So along walked Dalis, Alfonzo, Crooked Curt, Elizabeth, and Sasha, each looking a little less sad and lonely.

"Oh, my!" Dalis said, as she came upon three small furry animals.

"Who are you?" Dalis asked.

"I am Valentino the guinea pig. I was bought for a little girl who got bored with me."

"I'm Hollywood the ferret. I was bought for a little boy who thought I was too stinky."

"I'm Stew the bunny. I was bought as an Easter present for a family."

"And now we are no longer wanted," they all said. "What should we do?"

"Well," Dalis said, "Alfonzo has a broken leg, Crooked Curt has a disability, Elizabeth is very sick, Sasha needs a new home, and you three need a place to live as well. Come along with us, and I'll see how I can help."

So the animals followed Dalis back to her house, each looking a little less sad and lonely. When Dalis got home, she called her good buddy, Dr. KC, at the animal hospital where Dalis sometimes volunteered.

Dr. KC told Dalis to bring her new friends in right away. He fixed Alfonzo's broken leg, helped Crooked Curt with his disability, and gave Elizabeth medicine to make her healthy. He checked over Sasha, Valentino, Hollywood, and Stew to make sure they were healthy too.

Before Dalis took her new friends home, Dr. KC told her that if she were going to keep the animals, it was important for her to learn as much as she could about each animal.

Dalis went straight home and read about dogs, cats, lizards, birds, guinea pigs, ferrets, and bunnies. She learned a lot! She learned what all the animals need, and how to properly care for them.

She learned how long they live, what they eat, if they are cold-blooded, and even how important spaying and neutering are.

Dalis learned that Alfonzo needs to be walked every day, and that dogs need food that is made just for them. She also learned about how to safely approach other dogs by letting them first sniff her hand. Best of all, dogs love to play and cuddle.

Dalis learned a lot about cats too. She learned that some cats do not like to be picked up. She practiced letting Crooked Curt come to her when he was ready.

Cats also need special food made just for them to stay healthy.

Dalis also learned how important it is to clean Crooked Curt's litter box every day.

Dalis loved it when Crooked Curt purred to tell her he was happy.

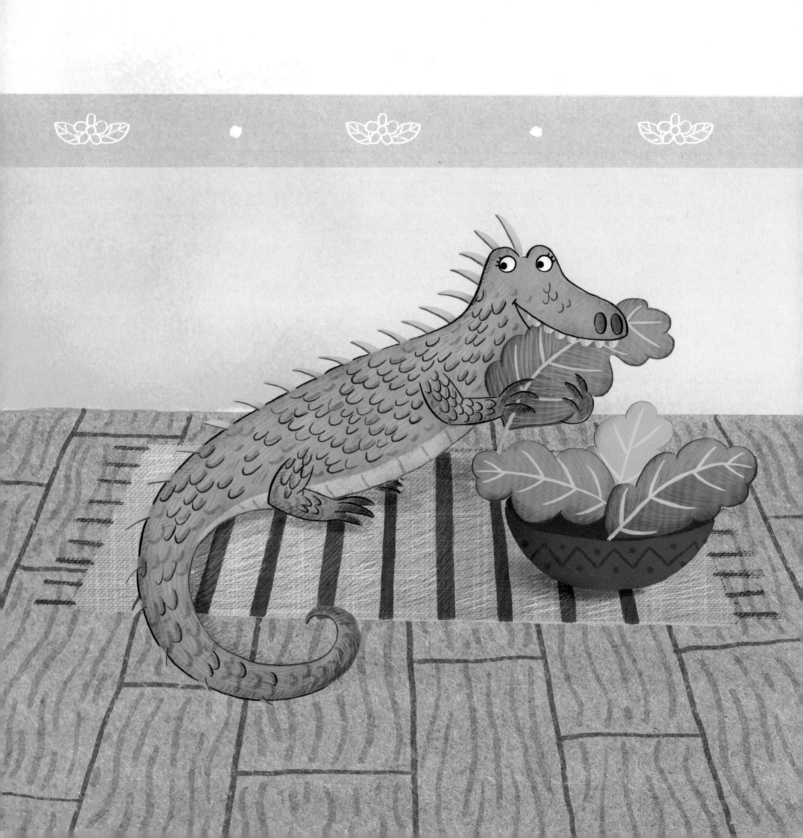

Dalis learned how to take care of Elizabeth and other reptiles too. Reptiles are cold-blooded animals. This means they need a warm and humid environment to survive.

Iguanas can get very big, so Elizabeth needed a large space of her own. Dalis and her mom bought a large glass enclosure and added a warming light and fresh water to keep Elizabeth healthy and happy. Elizabeth liked to eat fresh fruits and vegetables.

Dalis learned that even though animals like guinea pigs, bunnies, and ferrets are small, they need just as much care as other pets. Valentino, Hollywood, and Stew each needed a cage that was the right fit for them, and they need fresh water to drink and proper food to eat.

Dalis learned that Sasha is a cockatoo and that birds come in all shapes and sizes. Birds can be very messy and loud! But they are really intelligent, and Dalis had a lot of fun teaching her bird new tricks. Sasha's favorite toy was her bell, and her favorite trick was to dance.

After everything she learned, Dalis decided the only way to help animals like her new friends was to teach people the importance of animal care and how to keep pets healthy and happy.

Alfonzo, Crooked Curt, Elizabeth, Sasha, Valentino, Hollywood, and Stew shouted with excitement, "Dalis to the Rescue!"

Once the animals were all fixed up, healthy, and happy, Dalis decided to take all of the animals on the road with her to educate the humans. The animals learned that when Dalis put on her special shoes, it was time to go and teach people how to properly care for animals. Showtime!

Meet the Team!

All of the animals portrayed in the book are based on real animals, and Dalis is based on a real person too! Just like Dalis in the story, the real Dalis Hitchcock has been rescuing and advocating for animals most of her life. Alfonzo, Crooked Curt, Elizabeth, Sasha, Valentino, Hollywood, and Stew are all animals that Dalis rescued. She often takes her animal friends with her when she visits schools and groups to educate them about animals and pet ownership. Dalis to the rescue!

photo by Charis Seed Photography

Facts and Words to Know

Amphibians/Reptiles

All reptiles are amphibians. Amphibians are cold-blooded animals and need a warm and/or humid environment to thrive. Mammals, such as cats, dogs, and people, are warm-blooded and can regulate their own body temperatures. Reptiles rely on their environment to stay warm.

Facts

- Iguanas can grow to 4–6 feet and need a lot of space, such as a large glasslike enclosure.
- Iguanas can live 10–20 years if they are cared for properly. If iguanas are not well taken care of, they can get very sick and develop a metabolic bone disease and die.
- Seventy percent of store-bought iguanas die in the first year because the owners were not well-educated about caring for them.
- Reptiles can be very expensive and difficult to care for, and it is important to research how to properly care for them.

Birds

Birds can be loud and messy, but they are very intelligent. They require a lifetime commitment from their owner. They get bored easily and need lots of toys and attention to keep them occupied. Make sure there is an avian vet in your area before adopting or purchasing a bird as they will need lots of things done to keep them healthy, such as having their nails clipped and their beaks trimmed.

Facts

- Small birds, such as parakeets and lovebirds, can live 10–15 years. Large birds like Sasha and other macaws and cockatoos can live 40–60 years!
- Birds are very intelligent. The more time someone spends with them, the more a bird will learn.
- Birds eat a varied diet of pellets, whole raw foods such as vegetables, and cooked whole grains such as brown rice. Seeds should only make up 10–20 percent of their diets.

Facts

- Declawing, when a cat's claws are surgically removed, can cause behavioral problems, such as refusing to use the litter box or aggressive biting.
- When cats are fed a poor diet, they are more susceptible to urinary tract infections, which can lead to litter-box problems. The urinary tract is the part of the cat that helps it to urinate.

Cats

Cats are one of the largest animal populations in shelters. Cats can produce multiple litters of kittens quickly if they are not spayed and neutered. This can create lots and lots of abandoned and homeless cats. Older cats are at a higher risk of not being adopted because most people want to adopt kittens. If you are interested in adopting a cat, consider adopting an older cat. They are often calmer, and if healthy, cats can live a long time.

Dogs

The safest way to approach an unfamiliar dog is to first ask the owner if it's okay to pet the dog. If the owner says yes, then first let the dog sniff the back of your hand. This tells the dog who you are and that you are friendly. If you see a dog without an owner, do not approach the dog. Dogs need to walk and play every day. Teach your dog how to walk with a leash. Leashes help keep your dog and everyone else safe.

Facts

- Different breeds of dogs have different personalities. Make sure you research breeds so you will know which type of dog is the best fit for your family.
- Dogs need food made just for them. Table scraps and "people food" are not necessarily healthy for dogs.

Small Animals

In *Dalis to the Rescue*, Dalis rescues a guinea pig, a bunny, and a ferret. These are considered small animals. They require special care to say healthy and happy.

Facts

- Guinea pigs can live an average of 5–7 years.
- Guinea pigs are very social animals and are happiest when they live with other guinea pigs.
- Guinea pigs are one of the few animals (humans are another) that cannot produce their own vitamin C, so they need a proper diet to ensure they get all the vitamins they need to stay healthy.

- Bunnies (rabbits) live approximately 1–2 years in the wild but in captivity can live 8–12 years. It's important to also spay and neuter bunnies.
- Rabbits' nails and teeth never stop growing, so they need plenty of things to scratch and chew on to keep their nails and teeth from overgrowing.

- Ferrets live 6–10 years and sleep 17–20 hours a day.
- Ferrets need around 4 hours outside of their cage every day, and owners will need to "ferret-proof" their house.
- The name "ferret" is derived from the Latin word for "thief."
- Ferrets have a distinct musky odor that comes from their skin glands and is present whether the ferret is de-scented or not.

Other Words to Know

Euthanize

Euthanize means to humanely end an animal's life. When there are too many pets and not enough homes, animal shelters run out of room and have to euthanize animals.

Facts

- Approximately 670,000 dogs are euthanized every year.
- 860,000 cats are euthanized every year.

Spay/Neuter

Pets should be spayed and neutered. *Spay* (for female animals) and *neuter* (for male animals) means to sterilize pets so they can no longer reproduce. This is important because more than a million dogs and cats are euthanized every year.

Facts

- Two cats and their offspring can reproduce 420,000 kittens in seven years.
- It is important to also spay and neuter bunnies. Animal shelters take in more bunnies than any other type of animals after dogs and cats.

DALIS HITCHCOCK was born in Alma, Michigan, but her family moved around a lot when she was young. This meant that Dalis had to move from school to school, which made it hard for her to make friends and to find her place in the world. She turned to animals for friendship, and this is when the rescuing began! Dalis would save cats from trees, garter snakes from holes in the ground, and any other animals that needed rescuing.

Eventually her family moved back to Michigan and another new school, and Dalis felt left out all over again. Animals continued to be her constant source of companionship throughout her childhood, and as an adult, she opened her own dog and cat grooming salon in St. Louis, Michigan.

She soon started to see a need to help abandoned animals and to educate the public about the realities of pet adoption and ownership, so she created "Dalis to the Rescue." She has saved thousands of animals since including dogs, cats, birds, lizards, and small animals. She travels all over Michigan encouraging people to research animals before adopting, and educating them about proper animal care and the importance of spaying and neutering. She works seven days a week with the hopes that she can make a difference.

VERONICA MONTOYA was born in Alicante, a small beach city in the southeast of Spain. She studied Fine Arts in Valencia in the specialties of drawing and engraving. She now lives in a small town and works in her studio by the sea where she takes long walks with her dog, finds inspiration in nature, reads all kinds of books, listens to the radio, and illustrates books for everyone from ages 0 to 100.